...SO THE ARCHMAGE TRIMIC BURNT UP THE AETHER 'ROUND THE BATTLEFIELD TRYIN' TO STOP THE REBELS, BUT HE DIDN'T EXPECT—
EMBRYLL, LOOK! DRUKHOVI!
MAGNIFICENT.
THE STORIES REALLY DON'T DO IT JUSTICE.
I'LL JUST FINISH THAT TALE ANOTHER TIME.

SO THEY BUILT THIS WHOLE CITY AROUND A BIG SKELETON...
THE ELVES VANQUISHED DRUKHOVI THE VAST THOUSANDS OF YEARS AGO. AS THEY TELL IT, HE WAS ACTUALLY THE FIRST DRAGON, AS ANCIENT AS THE WORLD ITSELF...
THE DRAGON'S DEATH BIRTHED NEW LIFE; A MASSIVE, UNIQUE ECOSYSTEM UNLIKE ANYTHING IN CATALINE.
TRULY SPECTACULAR.
HEY, DO YOU HEAR THAT?
HRN? NO, BUT YER ELVEN EARS —ERR, EAR—— IS BETTER THAN MINE.
IT SOUNDS LIKE... MUSIC!
WAIT, DU—— HE'S GONE.

WHAAAAAAAAAAAAAAAAAAAAAAAAAAT!

HEY KID! WHAT'S GOING ON?
GOLLY, MISTER! IT'S DRUKHOVIFEST!

THE CAPTAIN! DO YOU KNOW ABOUT DRUKHOVIFEST? IT'S MY FAVORITE!
HUFF PUFF HUFF PUFF
EYES ON THE PRIZE, LAD. WE NEED TO FIND THE ELVEN ARCHIVES.
CAN'T WE JUST CELEBRATE FOR A FEW— UH, HOW LONG IS THIS THING?
ANOTHER MONTH YET, AT LEAST.
NO.

WHOAH, THEY CAUGHT THAT?
FER ELVES OF DRUKHOVI, THERE'S NO GREATER PURPOSE THAN HUNTIN' BEASTS AND SLAYIN' MONSTERS.
AND THAT IS THEIR QUEEN.
WILD, EH EMBRYLL?
OH, RIGHT, TOO MANY PEOPLE AROUND.
SECRET. SHHHH
BUMP!

OOPS! SORRY.
WHO THE—?!
LISTEN YOU LITTLE TWERP.
I'M ABOUT TO...
HEY, HOW COMES YOU ONLY GOT ONE EAR?
I HAVE TWO EARS! BUT ONLY ONE IS AN ELF EAR, I'M A HALF-ELF.
ON MY MOTHER'S SIDE.
I DON'T—HIC—THINK THAT'S A THING.
HA HA HA HA
I LIKE YOU! YOU'RE FUNNY!
COME! I SPILLED MY DRINK, YOU CAN BUY ME A NEW ONE!

WE DON'T REALLY HAVE TIME FOR THIS, DUFF.
WHAT? HE ASKED SO NICELY! PLUS WE NEED TO, UH, GATHER INFORMATION?
MUNCH MUNCH
DRUKHOVIFEST!
NOT SURE THESE ARE THE INFORMIN' TYPES.
BUT MAYBE THE BARKEEP KNOWS SOMETHIN'.
GULP
DUNK!
'SCUSE ME, KIND SIR.
ZZZZZZZ
HUM
SORRY FOR BOTHERIN' YA. I'M TRYIN' TO FIND MY WAY TO THE ARCHIVES.
YOU COME ALL THE WAY TO DRUKHOVI DURING DRUKHOVIFEST AND WANT TO LOOK AT BOOKS?
DWARVES, AYE... IT'S NEAR THE FEMUR.
HA HA HA!
THE LEFT ONE.

THIS PLACE IS HUGE! AND EMPTY!
INDEED, THEY STARTED IT AS A MEANS TO DOCUMENT THEIR RECORDS, BUT SOON IT BECAME MUCH MORE ROBUST.
MUST BE SOMETHIN' HERE TO LEAD US TO THAT SORCERER. LETS GET TO LOOKIN'.
THIS ONE'S ABOUT THE MIGRATION PATTERN OF HUMMINGBEARS. IS THAT HELPFUL?
OH, UH, NO. WE'RE LOOKING FOR ANY MENTION OF ESEN RASP. WE NEED TO FIND WHERE HE'S BEEN HIDING.
EVERYTHING'S ABOUT MONSTERS, HUNTING, OR HUNTING MONSTERS.
ONE TRACK MIND, THESE ELVES.
SOME OF THEM ARE FUNNY, THOUGH! THIS ONE IS ABOUT A MAGICAL DAGGER. THAT'S CRAZY, RIGHT?
IMAGINE THAT!
DUFF!

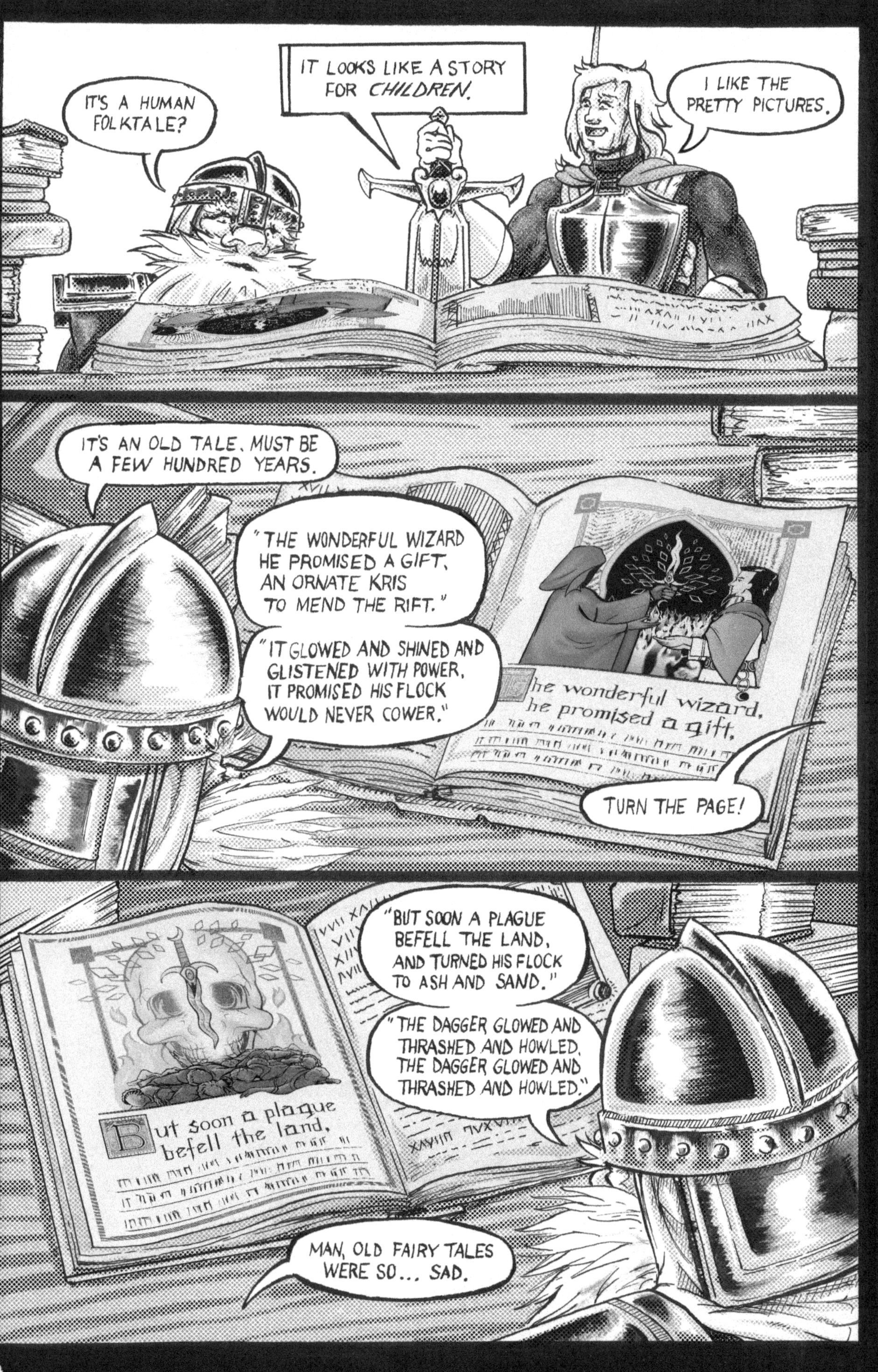

IT'S A HUMAN FOLKTALE?
IT LOOKS LIKE A STORY FOR CHILDREN.
I LIKE THE PRETTY PICTURES.
IT'S AN OLD TALE. MUST BE A FEW HUNDRED YEARS.
"THE WONDERFUL WIZARD HE PROMISED A GIFT, AN ORNATE KRIS TO MEND THE RIFT."
"IT GLOWED AND SHINED AND GLISTENED WITH POWER, IT PROMISED HIS FLOCK WOULD NEVER COWER."
he wonderful wizard, he promised a gift.
TURN THE PAGE!
"BUT SOON A PLAGUE BEFELL THE LAND, AND TURNED HIS FLOCK TO ASH AND SAND."
"THE DAGGER GLOWED AND THRASHED AND HOWLED, THE DAGGER GLOWED AND THRASHED AND HOWLED."
But soon a plague befell the land,
MAN, OLD FAIRY TALES WERE SO... SAD.

STRANGE. THIS LOOKS LIKE THE PLAGUE OF STONEFORT. BUT WHY IS IT IN A BOOK FOR LITTL' UNS?
THERE MUST BE MORE. FORGET THE HISTORY BOOKS; LOOK FOR FABLES, LULLABIES, FOLKLORE.
ATTACK OF THE BEASTMEN
TOM LESKO
HOW TO AVOID BEING EATEN BY A RATTERSNAKE
DOCTOR BAGS
WAGONHEAD
TONGUE
SIGNIFICANT HERO
WILLIAM WALTER
DR. CLOCKWISE AND THE HOURGLASS OF CHAOS
E. DUNK
TWILIGHT FISH MEMORIES
PATRICIA CORKIN
In the Claws of Romance
EXPERIMENTS IN LUNAPHAGE
KIND CONSULT
To Mock a Killingbird
E.E. Willis

BUTCHER LIKE AN ELF, EAT LIKE AN ORC
BUTCHER LIKE AN ELF, EAT LIKE AN ORC
R. G. SIRIUS
A VLAR'S TALE
Anilou
The Legend of the Belly Beans
WEAPONS OF WAR: HOW MAGIC SHAPED THE WAR OF THE NIGHT
CALLY LOTT
Getting the Most Out of Mage School
Denise Manson
THE NORTON BROTHERS' GUIDE TO MONSTER SLAYING
How to Hunt Snugglebears
Jerry Berry
Nivlac's Guide to Flexible Parenting
Cataloging the Indigenous Life of Swamp Monsters
ROBERT GRONT
Atlas of Southeast Cataline
101 Ways to Skin a Dragon
The Grabcyclopedia
Crescent, Demystified
TRAKK
How to Flay Your Dragon
Burpp
THE ALCHEMIST'S COOK BOOK
XIN
SWORD AND THE HEROES WHO WIELD
SWORDS AND THAT WIELD
The End of Magic?
Bank Ooru
In the Shadow of Crabs
The 1, 2, 3-ses of Diseases
The A, B, C-ses of Diseases
How to Scream So Monsters Will Listen & Listen So Monsters Will Scream
Alchemy in the Modern Era
MY LEAST FAVORITE MONSTERS: A - E
WHICH BATTLE AX TO USE: A GUIDE

BREAKABLE
BREA
WEAKNES
FAL·W AND SLAP?
possible transcription?
a lullaby ???
THEY'RE CAUTIONARY TALES, WOVEN
THROUGHOUT EVERY CULTURE'S HISTORY.
A STRANGER BEARS A MAGICAL GIFT...
FOLLOWED BY CATACLYSM. IT CANNOT
BE A COINCIDENCE. THIS IS ALL ESEN
RASP'S DOING. WE MUST STOP HIM.

soon a plag
efell the lanc
HEY THAT'S
YOU!

TSSSSSSS
HACK!
HUCK!
COUGH
KSHHH   KLANG
WHO ARE THESE LUNATICS?
THEY'RE TRYING TO STEAL MY SWORD!
THUNK

WHRAASH!!
KLANG!
HISSSSS
BUMP!!!
LIGHT BE, THERE'S TOO MANY OF THEM!
CRUNCH!
BOMF
UH?
EH?
WHA?

KZZZt
HI.
ARE YOU ON OUR SIDE, OR DO YOU JUST HAVE REALLY BAD AIM?
BOTH!
STOP THAT.
KLING
THANK YA KINDLY, BUT THESE FOLK STILL GOT SOME FIGHT IN 'EM.
CONKLE DONK!

GET DOWN!
BOOM.
ARE YOU SURE YOU'RE ON OUR SIDE?

HALT!
WHAT'S GOING ON IN HERE?
THESE BRIGANDS ATTACKED US!
I WAS DEFENDING THESE INNOCENT PEOPLE!
I'M ACTUALLY A GUARD, TOO!
KLINK!!!
I CAN'T BELIEVE...
MY CONCOCTIONS WORKED SO WELL!

I HAD NO IDEA THAT REPLACING THE SNUGGLEBEAR BLADDER WITH A PULSEFROG SPLEEN WOULD INCREASE THE RADIUS BY THAT MUCH.
IT WAS AT LEAST 10% MORE IMPACTFUL.
? ? ?
? ? ?
I NEED TO WRITE THIS DOWN...
POP!
POP!
OH, I SHOULD...
HI. I'M GWYNN LOREMIR.
NICE TA MEE—
AND YOU'RE THE CAPTAIN, AND HE'S DUFFENDRYLL YLLALYNN.
WE'VE BEEN FOLLOWING YOU!
WHAT YA MEAN "WE?"
YES, "WE."
SALUTATIONS! I AM SYNADOR THE MAGNIFYCENT, BUT YOU CAN JUST CALL ME SYNADOR THE SPLENDID.
OR JUST SYNADOR I SUPPOSE.

WHOAH! YOUR STAFF CAN TALK?!
HA, OH, WHY HELLO THERE, HEHEHE.
DID YOU FIND IT AFTER A MYSTERIOUS EXPLOSION CAUSED A SINKHOLE INTO A LOST UNDERGROUND CITY?
NO. THAT'S VERY SPECIFIC.
SEVERAL MONTHS AGO I WAS COLLECTING ALCHEMICAL MATERIALS NEAR THE MAGI MEMORIAL CEMETERY WHEN I FOUND SYNADOR IN ONE OF THE TOMBS.
WHAT KINDA MATERIALS WERE YA COLLECTIN' NEAR A CEME—
TEETH.
SYNADOR AND I HAVE BEEN WORKING TOGETHER. HE BELIEVES THERE MAY BE OTHER WEAPONS LIKE HIM.
...AND HE IS NOT MISTAKEN.
IT'S THE SWORD!
AMAZING. I THOUGHT IT'D BE THE CAPTAIN'S AX.
I TOLD YOU IT WAS THE SWORD.

I'M EMBRYLL. DUFF RESCUED ME FROM BENDARIN. YOU WERE NEAR STONEFORT?
INDEED! ONCE I GRACED THE HAND OF THE ILLUSTRIOUS ORIA AGENFORN, THE FAMED GNOMISH SCHOLAR! I WAS GIFTED UNTO HIM BY THE TRAVELING MAGI ESEN RASP, RIGHT BEFORE THE STORMS BEGAN.
AND YOU?
I WAS RASP'S GIFT TO THE KING AND QUEEN OF BENDARIN BEFORE THE "EARTHQUAKE."
WE'VE FOUND EVIDENCE THAT THE SORCEROR VISITED THE ELVES, DWARVES, HUMANS, GNOMES, ORCS, AND DRAGLINGS ALL AROUND THE SAME TIME NEARLY 500 YEARS AGO.
ALL OF THEM? RIGHT BEFORE THE DEVASTATION?
THAT DOESN'T SOUND LIKE A COINCIDENCE.
SQUADALA...
IT'S WORSE THAN THAT. HE'S CAUSING NEW EARTHQUAKES IN BENDARIN. THEY'RE DESTROYING OVERMINE!
SHICK

BUT THE AETHER IS GONE. MAGIC THAT POTENT... HOW IS IT POSSIBLE?
I FELT HIS POWER IN BENDARIN, HE IS RESPONSIBLE—I'M SURE OF IT.
I SENSE IT HERE, TOO. WHEN I'M NEAR SYNADOR, IT'S AS IF I'M BEING PULLED SOMEWHERE, EVER SO SLIGHTLY.
LIKE AN INDECIPHERABLE WHISPER; TOO QUIET TO DISCERN, TOO LOUD TO DISMISS.
MAYBE IF WE FIND THE OTHER WEAPONS RASP MADE, YOU CAN LEAD US STRAIGHT TO HIM!
AMAZING, DUFF! YOU ARE BRILLIANT. WE MUST GATHER THE REST.
WE FIND IT ODD THEY LET US KEEP OUR WEAPONS?
SORRY TO INTERRUPT, USUALLY FIRST THING GUARDS DO IS DISARM YA. THEY DIDN'T BOTHER. SEEMS OFF.
MAYBE THEY... FORGOT?
I DON'T THINK THEY FORGOT.
TAKE A LOOK.

ONLY THE BRAVEST WARRIORS WILL SURVIVE... PROVE YOUR STRENGTH AND EARN YOUR FREEDOM IN THE WYRMBONE COLOSSEUM!
SSSSSLAP!
OH MAN! WHO DO YOU THINK IS GOING TO FIGHT NEXT?